REINDEER DOWN!

An Irish Christmas Tale

Natasha Mac a'Bháird

ILLUSTRATED by Audrey Dowling

THE O'BRIEN PRESS
DUBLIN

dication

Natasha: To my lovely nieces and nephews - Leo, Donnchadh, Jacob, Aoife and Alannah.

Audrey: To Paul, for his unwavering faith in me.

First published 2019 by The O'Brien Press Ltd,
12 Terenure Road East, Rathgar, Dublin 6, D06 HD27, Ireland
Tel: +353 1 4923333; Fax: +353 1 4922777
E-mail: books@obrien.ie
Website: www.obrien.ie
The O'Brien Press is a member of Publishing Ireland.

6 5 4 3 2 1
21 20 19

Printed and bound in Poland by Białostockie Zakłady Graficzne S.A.
The paper used in this book is produced using pulp from managed forests.

Published in

DUBLIN
UNESCO
City of Literature

'That's right, Rudolph!' called Santa.
'Full speed ahead!
We're nearly in Ireland!'

EIRE

Santa and the reindeer were having a busy night.
They had been to lots of different countries and
delivered thousands of presents.

Now they were high in the sky above the
Atlantic Ocean, with stars twinkling above
and waves crashing below.

Rory, the smallest reindeer, sat at the back of the sleigh.
He peered out, excited to see Ireland for the first time.

Rory was Rudolph's son.
It was his first sleigh trip.
It was his job to help Santa sort
all the presents and make sure
no one was forgotten.

'We're nearly there!' Rory cried.

Quick as a twinkle, Santa's sleigh passed the Giant's Causeway.

The reindeer slowed down as the sleigh flew towards the first house.

The sleigh landed with a bump on the rooftop.

But instead of coming
to a gentle stop it
started sliding along
the roof. Rory clutched
the edge in fright.
What was going on?

"Whoa, whoa!" called Santa. The reindeer seemed to be getting into a tangle! Santa pulled on the reins, but he couldn't stop the sleigh sliding forward.

Rory felt another bump.
The sleigh had crashed into Dancer!

Santa jumped out of the sleigh. Rory rushed to help.
Poor Dancer had got a real bang from the sleigh.

'Oh dear, oh dear,' Santa said as he helped her up.

Cupid came over to see what she could do.
Dancer had a big bump on her hind leg and looked very pale.

'You have a little rest, Dancer,' Rudolph said. 'Rory, can
you see if the children have left out something for us?'

Rory bounded forward, eager to help.
Santa sprinkled magic dust on him.
He shrank down until he was small
enough to fit down the chimney.

Rory loved when Santa let him go down the chimney.
Usually he couldn't wait to see the beautiful Christmas
tree and the treats the children had left out.
But now he was too worried about Dancer to feel excited.

Whoosh! Rory was back on the rooftop with some
carrots and a mince pie for Santa.
'Give Dancer a mince pie, too,' Santa said.

Dancer was very grateful and gobbled them up.

While Santa left out his presents, Rory filled the children's stockings. The older reindeer waited anxiously to see if Dancer would feel better.

'I'll be fine,' the brave reindeer insisted, but Rudolph and Cupid were very worried. When Santa came back up the chimney he went to talk to them.

'Dancer has got a bad bang on her leg,' Rudolph told Santa.
'I don't know if she'll be able to fly,' Cupid said.

'Oh dear,' said Santa. 'We still have a lot of presents left and
the sleigh is very heavy. I really need all of you to pull it.'

'Let me help, Santa!' said Rory eagerly. 'I'm really big and strong!' He stood up on his hind legs to show Santa just how big he was.

'I know you are, Rory, but I need you to help with the presents,' Santa said. 'I don't want to get mixed up!'

'I'm fine, really!' Dancer said bravely.

'Maybe you should have a longer rest,' suggested Cupid.

'No, let's keep going!' Dancer insisted.

'Well, if you're sure,' Santa replied doubtfully.

'All right then – away we go!'

The sleigh soared into the sky passing Lough Neagh and the Mourne Mountains. Soon Santa was very busy sorting presents while Rory ticked them off the list, filling lots of stockings with presents.

Rory was worried about Dancer. She was flying with her sore leg tucked up. She looked very tired. 'Santa, I don't think Dancer can fly for much longer,' he whispered loudly.

Dancer heard and burst into tears.
'I'm trying my best, but I don't think I'll be able to make it all the way back to the North Pole.'

'Don't worry, Dancer,' Santa reassured her.
'We'll think of something.'

Then Rory had a brilliant idea. 'I know!
What about our friends in the Phoenix Park?
I'm sure they would be happy to help.'

'Of course!' said Santa. 'Why didn't I think of that?
Full speed ahead to Dublin!'
The sleigh raced past Newgrange towards Dublin,

The Phoenix Park was cold and beautiful in the winter
moonlight. Rory was so excited when he heard the
wolves howl as they flew over Dublin Zoo.

Leading the other reindeer, Rudolph looked all around for
their friends.

There they are!' shouted Rory, spotting the herd of fallow deer grazing by the Wellington Monument.

'Down we go!' said Santa. 'Easy now!'

The sleigh landed with a gentle bump.
Straight away they were surrounded by the fallow deer.

'Santa, it's so good to see you!' Fergus cried.
'What are you doing here?' Fia asked.
'We thought you'd be busy delivering presents.'

Santa explained about Dancer's injury. 'So you see, we need someone to take over from Dancer.'

'Oh, let me help!' begged Fia. 'I'd love to pull the sleigh.'
'Very well,' said Santa. 'But what will we do about Dancer?'

'Leave Dancer here with us,' said Fergus. 'We'll take care of her until she feels better.'

'Thank you,' said Santa. 'I'm glad to know Dancer will be well looked after. Have a good rest, Dancer! I'll send the elves to check on you next week.'

Dancer was happy to stay and rest with their kind friends. Rory was very excited to have Fia helping to pull the sleigh. He was looking forward to showing her the North Pole!

Santa sprinkled magic dust over Fia. He called out to the reindeer. Once again the sleigh rose into the sky, ready to continue its very important journey.

Dancer relaxed with the other deer, glad that she would have a good week's rest before she had to fly home.

So if you happen to be in the Phoenix Park, look out for a reindeer who looks just a little bit different from the other deer.

If you hide behind a tree so you won't be spotted, you might even see some of Santa's elves coming to check on her!